HOW THE LION LOST HIS LUNCH
LUNCH
Adventures with Jeremy James

A hungry lion is not the only unusual inhabitant of Warkin-on-Sea. Jeremy James also encounters a non-go, non-stop donkey, a lady who hates children, a totty-botty man, and monkeys who eat cars.

HOW THE LION LOST HIS LUNCH

David Henry Wilson

Illustrated by Axel Scheffler

CHIVERS PRESS
BATH

First published 1980 under the title
Beside the Sea with Jeremy James by
Chatto & Windus Ltd
This Large Print edition published by
Chivers Press
by arrangement with
the author
1997

ISBN 0 7451 6973 2

British Library Cataloguing in Publication Data

Wilson, David Henry, 1937–
    How the lion lost his lunch. — Large print ed. — (Adventures
with Jeremy James ; 3)
    1. Children's stories, English   2. Large type books
    I. Title   II. Scheffler, Axel   III. Beside the sea with Jeremy
James
    823.9'14[J]

ISBN 0 7451 6973 2

CONTENTS

For my father,
and in loving memory of my mother

CHAPTER ONE

GOING AWAY

Mummy had spent the morning cooking, cleaning the house, dressing Christopher and Jennifer, and packing suitcases. Daddy had spent the morning putting the roof rack on the car. It was a very difficult roof rack to put on, as Daddy kept explaining to Mummy when he came in for a breather, for a screwdriver, or for sticking plaster. It was one of those roof racks which had a mind of its own. If one side was straight, the other was crooked, and if Daddy straightened out the crooked side, then the other side would go crooked. And when both sides were finally straight, the clamps got themselves hidden. And when Mummy found the clamps, it was the screws that got hidden ... It really was a difficult roof rack to put on.

Jeremy James tried to help Daddy at first, by holding things for him. Daddy had said, 'We'll soon have this job done,' and Jeremy James had stood there holding things for hours and hours, until eventually Mummy had said he should go and play, while Daddy fixed the roof rack on his own.

All these activities were in preparation for the holiday. There had been an unusual spell of summer sunshine—two days in succession—and the weather forecast had promised more. Mummy had said she could do with a break, and Jeremy James said he could do with a break as well, and as Daddy had nothing urgent to think about doing, they decided to spend a week at the seaside. The day was in fact rather grey and cloudy, but Daddy said it was bound to clear up soon. That was just before he said he'd get the roof rack on soon. But even after the roof rack was on, the day was still grey and cloudy.

'Don't you think you'd better cover the cases?' said Mummy.

'Oh no, it'll brighten up soon,' said Daddy. 'That's what the weather forecast said.'

'Hmmph,' said Mummy. 'I still think you should cover the cases.'

And so Daddy covered the cases. It took him quite a while to cover the cases, and it took quite a while for Mummy to finish sticking bits of plaster on Daddy, but at last the car was loaded and they were all set to leave.

'Have you done a wee?' Mummy asked Jeremy James.

'No, I don't feel like it,' said Jeremy James.

'Go upstairs and do one all the same,' said Mummy.

Jeremy James went upstairs, didn't do a wee, and came downstairs again.

'There's a good boy,' said Mummy.

'Hmmph,' said Jeremy James.

Then they all went out to the car.

Christopher and Jennifer were comfortably bedded down in their pram-top at the back, Jeremy James was strapped into his seat, Mummy sat next to Jeremy James so that she could reach the twins, and Daddy was alone at the front. With a whirr, a cough and a roar the engine started first time, and away they went.

'It's started to rain,' said Mummy.

'So it has,' said Daddy. 'Good job I covered the cases.'

It seemed strange to be leaving the house behind. Jeremy James looked back. The windows were closed, the doors were locked, and the upstairs curtains were drawn, as if somehow the house had gone to sleep. Jeremy James waved.

'Who are you waving to?' asked Mummy.

'The house,' said Jeremy James. 'It'll be lonely without us.'

They were soon driving through the town, and Jeremy James enjoyed looking out of the window at the cars, shops and people. Everything was very wet now, because it was raining quite

4

heavily, but inside the car it was warm and dry, which somehow made the journey even more exciting. Jeremy James wondered if all the people outside had realized that this particular car was going on a special journey. He tried to see their faces, and in fact quite a few people did seem to look at the car as it passed by. One or two even pointed, and Jeremy James felt very pleased that they had noticed the particular car going on its special journey.

'We are important,' said Jeremy James. 'People are looking at us.'

At that very moment there was a loud flapping noise, and something fell down over the window, shutting out all the people who had been looking at the important car.

'Oh Lord,' said Daddy, 'it's the tarpaulin.'

The car squealed to a halt, and despite some angry hoots from behind, Daddy jumped out into the pouring rain. Then the car shook and rocked and trembled as Daddy fought with the tarpaulin. Judging by the way Daddy kept rushing round the car, the tarpaulin seemed to be winning, but after a while some raincoated chests and stomachs pressed up against the windows on either side. A voice shouted, 'Have you got it?' and another voice shouted, 'We're all right this side!' and then more voices joined in and more chests and stomachs shut out the rain and the light. Then the car stopped shaking, and the door opened. With cries of 'Thanks very much!' and 'Cheerio!' and 'Do the same for you one day!' Daddy dropped, or rather dripped, into his seat and closed the door.

'Phew,' he said. 'Blooming cases are all soaked through.'

'And so are you,' said Mummy. 'Here, dry yourself with this.'

She passed Daddy a nappy from the back of the car. Daddy looked at it closely.

'Hasn't been used, has it?' he asked.

Mummy laughed and shook her head, and Daddy rubbed his hair and face with the nappy.

'There we are,' he said, handing it back. 'Dry as a baby's bottom. Let's hope I shan't get nappy rash all over my face.'

There were more hoots from behind, and when Jeremy James looked through the rear window, he could see a whole line of cars and buses and lorries. In fact the man in the car behind was just getting out when Daddy said, 'Away we go!' and away they went, squirting a jet of water right up into the face of the man, who shook his fist in the air.

'No patience, some people,' said Daddy, as they cruised through the High Street. 'Remarkably traffic-free for this time of day.'

'I think they're all behind us, dear,' said Mummy. 'That's why they were hooting.'

The rain was coming down even heavier now, and the windscreen wipers clicked out a jolly rhythm as they swished across the glass.

'I thought you said it was going to clear up soon,' said Mummy.

'*I* didn't say it,' said Daddy. 'The weather men said it. They promised fine weather for today.'

'Do you know the men in charge of the weather?' asked Jeremy James, gazing with new admiration at the back of

Daddy's head.

'No,' said Daddy.

'Oh,' said Jeremy James, not quite so admiringly.

'And they don't know me,' said Daddy. 'And what's more, they don't know the weather either.'

But in spite of the rain, Jeremy James found it very exciting to be going on holiday, and when they drove on to the motorway, the adventure became even more thrilling. Everyone was racing along, and even Daddy's car managed to overtake some lorries, as well as an occasional car (usually driven by an old lady). Jeremy James pretended that it was a motor race, and every time they overtook someone, it brought them one place nearer the front. He didn't count the times that people overtook them, because those people were in a different race which he called the lunatics' race, as Daddy said they were all lunatics. The real race was between Daddy's car and everything else in the slow and middle lanes. Sometimes there would be a slow car in the middle lane (a slow car was one that went slower than Daddy's), and

8

Daddy would call the driver a middle-lane-hugger who shouldn't be allowed on the motorway. Once, when they passed a middle-lane-hugger, Jeremy James looked back at the driver's face, and he saw the man's lips move to form a word which might just possibly have been 'lunatic'.

'These people shouldn't be allowed on the motorway,' said Daddy. Then he pulled over to leave the way clear for a big black car which had been following them with its headlights flashing.

'Lunatic!' said Daddy as the big black car raced by.

Perhaps it was the excitement, or perhaps it was the influence of the rain streaming down from the sky, or perhaps it was simply the delayed effect of the orange juice at breakfast—but whatever the cause, Jeremy James suddenly became aware of a feeling. It was a feeling that would not go away. And it was a feeling that soon became very strong and very urgent.

'I want to do a wee,' said Jeremy James.

The announcement was not greeted

9

with any enthusiasm from Mummy or from Daddy. Mummy merely said, 'Oh!' and Daddy used his lunatic or middle-lane-hugger voice to inquire: 'Can't you wait?'

'No,' said Jeremy James, 'it's coming.'

'You'd better pull over to the side,' said Mummy. 'Let him do it on the verge.'

'You're not supposed to stop,' said Daddy. 'Except in an emergency.'

Jeremy James wriggled in his seat.

'It *is* an emergency,' said Mummy.

Daddy pulled over on to the hard shoulder, and Mummy unstrapped Jeremy James. She quickly put a raincoat on him, and Daddy got out of the car and came round to open Jeremy James's door. They just got to the grass verge in time.

They were about to walk back to the car, when there was a flashing of lights and a squealing of brakes, and there beside them was a real live police car. Out of the police car came two real live policemen, who stood in front of Jeremy James and Daddy as if they had just stepped out of the television screen.

'What's the trouble, sir?' asked the taller of the two policemen.

'Waterworks,' said Daddy.

'In the engine, sir?' asked the policeman.

'In my little boy,' said Daddy.

'Oh!' said the policeman. 'You know you're not supposed to stop on the motorway, don't you, sir?'

'Yes, I realize that,' said Daddy. 'But it was an emergency.'

'You ought to have driven to the nearest exit,' said the policeman.

'My little boy couldn't wait,' said Daddy.

The tall policeman looked very serious, and Jeremy James began to feel rather worried. He knew you weren't supposed to steal, or to kill people, but perhaps there was also a special law that you mustn't wee-wee on motorways. He gazed up at the tall policeman.

'You're not going to put us in prison, are you?' he asked.

The tall policeman looked down at Jeremy James, and then he looked across at the other policeman, who had a round red face that was suddenly covered by a

12

wide grin. The tall policeman crouched down so that he wasn't quite so far away from Jeremy James.

'Do you think we should?' he asked.

'Oh no,' said Jeremy James. 'I didn't know you weren't allowed to wee on motorways.'

'You're not allowed to *stop* on motorways,' said the policeman.

'Oh,' said Jeremy James, 'but I don't think I could wee without stopping.'

The other policeman laughed out loud, and the tall one stood up and patted Jeremy James on the head.

'On your way then,' he said. 'And try not to let it happen again.'

'Have a good holiday,' said the second policeman. 'Hope the weather clears up for you.'

Daddy looked up at the sky. 'You wouldn't think so,' he said, 'but according to the weather men, the sun's shining now.'

'I expect it is, sir,' said the second policeman. 'Just behind those black clouds.'

Mummy strapped Jeremy James into his seat again, and as they drove off,

Jeremy James turned and waved to the two policemen. They waved back, and climbed into their car beneath the flashing light.

'Well, that was nice,' said Jeremy James, feeling very pleased with himself.

'Delightful,' said Daddy, as they rejoined the lunatics and the middle-lane-huggers. 'The perfect start to a holiday.'

'And all thanks to me,' said Jeremy James.

CHAPTER TWO

MRS GULLICK

At first Warkin-on-Sea looked exactly the same as the town at home. The roads were the same, the houses were the same, the shops were the same, and the people were the same. And when Daddy stalled the engine at the traffic lights ('Something wrong with the worple worple,' said Daddy), Jeremy James was sure it was the same man hooting from behind who had hooted at them in the rain at home. But when Daddy drove down to the sea front, Jeremy James felt a lot happier. Because the sea front was completely different from any place Jeremy James had ever seen. On one side there were open-fronted shops, cafés, and yum-yummy ice cream parlours. On the other there were stretches of green, with flowers, and benches, and shelters. And beyond that was a wall which wasn't very high, and beyond the not very high wall was ... the sea. Jeremy

James could see it even from where he was—miles and miles of moving grey water, stretching as far as the eye could reach. There was enough water there for twenty million baths. If only it was lemonade, thought Jeremy James.

'Can I go in the sea?' he asked.

'Tomorrow,' said Mummy. 'It's getting late now—we must find a hotel.'

'Will we get ice creams as well?' asked Jeremy James.

'You'll have ice creams as well,' said Mummy.

'Oh look!' shouted Jeremy James. 'There's trampolines. Oh and swings ... it's a playground ...'

'You'll go to the playground too,' said Mummy.

'And there's a boating lake!' cried Jeremy James.

'Tomorrow,' said Mummy. 'You'll have plenty of time tomorrow.'

'Oh, can't I go today?' asked Jeremy James.

'We must find a hotel first,' said Mummy. 'Then if there's time after that, you can go.'

It was the old grown-up story: first

16

you must do what you don't want to do, and then if there's time you can do what you do want to do.

'Can't we go to the playground first?' he asked, but he knew they couldn't. Grown-ups never change, and Mummy was sure to say no.

'No,' said Mummy.

'I knew you'd say that,' said Jeremy James.

Finding a hotel proved to be a lot harder than expected. Daddy drove along the front, but all the hotels had notices up saying 'no vacancies', which apparently meant they were full. Jeremy James spotted a huge hotel on a hill and said he'd like to stay there, but Daddy said that was the Grand Metropolitan and had five stars, which must have meant that that was full as well. By the time Daddy had driven along the different side roads, round the squares, up the hills and down the dales, it looked as if they would have to go home even before Jeremy James had had a single ice cream, swing, bathe or boat.

They were on their way down towards the sea-front for the third or fourth time

17

when Daddy pointed towards an old house set back from the road behind some tall hedges.

'Might be worth a try,' he said. 'Come on, Jeremy James.'

Daddy and Jeremy James got out of the car, and Daddy opened the front gate. Behind the hedges was a large, overgrown garden, and completely hidden from the road was a notice which Daddy read out. It said:

GULLICK HOUSE
Bed and Breakfast
Proprietor Mrs M Gullick
VACANCIES

'Not "no vacancies"?' asked Jeremy James.

'Vacancies,' said Daddy. 'No "no". And no "no" means "yes". Let's go and see Mrs Gullick.'

They walked up the cracked concrete path to the flaking grey front door, and Daddy rang the bell.

Nothing happened for quite a long time, and Daddy was just raising his hand to ring again when the door

opened, and there stood a tall woman
with grey hair and a very serious face.
  'Yes?' she said.

'Mrs Gullick?' asked Daddy.

'Yes,' said Mrs Gullick.

'Ah,' said Daddy. 'Do you have a room suitable for me and my family? Apart from us, there's my wife and twin babies.'

'Babies,' said Mrs Gullick. 'I haven't got cots. I can't take babies.'

'We've got things they can sleep in,' said Daddy quickly. 'All we need is the room.'

'I've got a room for three,' said Mrs Gullick. 'But nothing for babies.'

'We'll take it,' said Daddy. 'A room for three'll be fine.'

'How long are you staying?' asked Mrs Gullick.

'Just one night,' said Daddy.

Jeremy James tugged at Daddy's coat. 'Not just one night, Daddy,' he said. 'We're staying for a whole week.'

Daddy looked at Jeremy James in the same way as he looked at roof racks and middle-lane-huggers, and then he turned to Mrs Gullick again. 'Um ... ah ...' he said, 'we're ... um ... travelling around, you see. Just one night in Warkin.'

'Then when can I go on the

20

trampolines and things?' asked Jeremy James.

'You'll have plenty of time for that,' said Daddy, in a Mummy-like that's-enough voice.

'I don't see how,' grumbled Jeremy James.

'Just one night, Mrs Gullick,' said Daddy.

'It'll be forty pounds,' said Mrs Gullick. 'And no breakfast for the babies.'

'Phew!' said Daddy.

'I don't usually have babies,' said Mrs Gullick.

'I'm not surprised,' said Daddy.

'And I like to be paid in advance,' said Mrs Gullick.

Daddy pulled out his wallet, and gave Mrs Gullick forty pounds. Then for the first time Mrs Gullick smiled. Jeremy James had never seen a smile quite like Mrs Gullick's smile. It wasn't jolly. It wasn't even friendly. It was simply a widening of the mouth across the surface of the face, more like a drawing of a smile than a real smile. And then she patted Jeremy James on the head, and it felt just like being patted with a dead fish.

'And what's your name?' she asked.

'Jeremy James,' said Jeremy James.

'You'll be a good boy, won't you?' said Mrs Gullick. 'Hm? You won't go putting dirty finger marks on the walls, will you?'

'No,' said Jeremy James.

'Or jumping on the furniture, or stamping on the floor.' She looked across at Daddy. 'We like to keep the house nice and quiet, you see,' she said.

'We'll be as quiet as we can,' said Daddy.

'That's right,' said Mrs Gullick. 'No shouting or screaming, hm, Jeremy James?'

'Well,' said Jeremy James, 'I might shout just a bit.'

'No, no,' said Mrs Gullick. 'If you're not a good boy, I shan't give you any breakfast.'

Jeremy James was about to point out that she *had* to give him breakfast because Daddy had *paid* for it, but Daddy took his hand and he found himself walking back towards the car.

'I don't like her,' said Jeremy James.

'She's creepy.'

'And that,' said Daddy, 'is why we're only staying here for one night.'

* * *

A few minutes later, the creepy Mrs Gullick was leading the family up three flights of steep, creepy stairs. The house was dark and musty, and the carpets were faded and worn. On each floor there were gloomy cupboards and tables, and vases without flowers, and on the walls there were old photographs in dull wooden frames. It was the sort of house that would have dead bodies in the cellar and ghosts in the attic. Jeremy James shuddered and took a quick look behind to make sure no one was following him up the stairs.

The room they were to sleep in *was* the attic. It contained a huge brown cupboard with a creaky door, a double bed with brass rails, a small bed with no rails, a dressing table with a cracked mirror, an armchair with a spring poking out of the seat, and a lot of little pictures round the walls—mainly photographs of old men and women.

'You'll be on your own up here,' said Mrs Gullick. 'The bathroom's along the corridor. Only a bath'll cost you extra.'

'What time's breakfast?' asked Daddy.

'Eight-thirty,' said Mrs Gullick.

'Till when?' asked Daddy.

'Just eight-thirty,' said Mrs Gullick.

'Ugh, that's a bit early,' said Daddy.

'It's the normal time,' said Mrs Gullick.

'Could I have some boiled water, please, Mrs Gullick?' asked Mummy.

'Sorry,' said Mrs Gullick. 'I only do breakfasts.'

'It's for the babies' feed,' said Mummy.

'Oh,' said Mrs Gullick. 'Boiled water. Well ... I don't take babies, you see ...'

'If you could just fill these two flasks for us,' said Mummy, in her do-as-you're-told voice.

Mrs Gullick went down the stairs, mumbling and muttering.

'What an awful woman,' said Mummy. 'And what an awful place.'

'We'll find a better place tomorrow,'

24

said Daddy. 'But this is the only one with vacancies.'

'I'd be surprised if it didn't have vacancies,' said Mummy.

*   *   *

Daddy and Jeremy James went to unload the car, while Mummy saw to the twins, both of whom were now wailing for their supper. When Daddy and Jeremy James had gone down and up the stairs for the third time, they found Mrs Gullick in the room.

'I don't usually have babies,' she was saying. 'They make a noise. I'm not used to them.'

'Haven't you any children of your own, Mrs Gullick?' asked Mummy.

'No,' said Mrs Gullick. 'I don't like children.'

This was too much for Jeremy James. He stood right in front of Mrs Gullick, looked straight up into her long, lined face, and said:

'If you don't like children, then children won't like you, so there!'

There was a stunned silence. Even

25

Mummy and Daddy were too surprised to say anything, and Mrs Gullick stood quite still and expressionless, like a vase without flowers. And then a very strange thing happened. Her face sort of crumpled, and her eyes grew moist, and she began to cry. It was silent crying, a bit like Mummy when she was peeling onions, but Jeremy James could clearly see two large teardrops trickling down the side of Mrs Gullick's nose.

'I'm sorry, Mrs Gullick,' said Daddy. 'He didn't mean it...'

'I did mean it,' said Jeremy James, rather more subdued. 'Only I didn't mean it so that you should cry.'

'You're quite right,' said Mrs Gullick. 'I must seem a rather nasty old woman to you.'

'Yes, you do,' said Jeremy James, a little surprised at Mrs Gullick's knowledge of his thoughts.

'Jeremy James, sh!' whispered Mummy.

'The truth is,' said Mrs Gullick, 'I did once have a little boy of my own. Only I lost him, you see.'

'Oh dear,' said Jeremy James.

'Couldn't you find him again?'

'No,' said Mrs Gullick, very softly. 'No, I never found him again. So it always makes me sad to see children.'

'Well, you should have had some more like Mummy did,' said Jeremy James.

Mrs Gullick put her hand on Jeremy James's shoulder, and as she looked down at him, her face seemed somehow kinder and gentler.

'I couldn't,' she said. 'You see, I lost my husband, too.'

'Oh,' said Jeremy James. 'You must be very careless, losing them both.'

Mummy came to Jeremy James's side.

'I think you've chattered enough now, Jeremy James,' she said. 'Why don't you help Daddy finish the unloading?'

'Come on, Jeremy James,' said Daddy. 'Let's get back to work.'

As they left the room, though, Jeremy James heard Mrs Gullick say to Mummy: 'What a lovely boy. You must be very proud of him.'

And when Mummy said yes, she was, Mrs Gullick said: 'My son's name was James too. And I'd have been proud if he'd been like your son.'

27

'You know,' said Jeremy James, as he and Daddy went out of the front door, 'I think Mrs Gullick's quite nice really. In fact, I think I like her after all.'

'Glad to hear it,' said Daddy. 'And I think she likes you, too.'

CHAPTER THREE

KERDOING

It was bedtime. The family had been to a restaurant in town for their supper, and faced with a limitless choice Jeremy James had chosen the most luxurious dish in the world: fish and chips. He had followed that up with strawberries and cream, and had accompanied the whole meal with a glass of cool Coca-Cola. Now he felt very full and rather sleepy.

The twins had been lively all evening, but after a lot of rocking and coaxing they had quietened down. Daddy was in his pyjamas and Mummy was in her nightdress, and Jeremy James had been tucked up in his bed. He felt really cosy. There was something warm and tingly about sleeping in the same room as Mummy, Daddy and the twins—as if they'd got a little world all to themselves.

Daddy stood by the door with his hand on the light switch, and Mummy climbed into bed.

29

'Kerdoing!' said the bed.

'Oh dear,' said Mummy. 'It's one of those.'

The bed gave another creak and groan as Mummy made herself comfortable. Then Daddy switched off the light, and Jeremy James heard him pad across the room.

'Kerdingadongadoing!' said the bed, and then it creaked and cracked and kerdoinged as if it was on the verge of falling to pieces.

'Oh Lord,' said Daddy. 'Can you move over a bit, love?'

'If I move over any more,' said Mummy, 'I'll fall out of the window.'

'Well, I'm right on the edge here,' said Daddy.

'And I'm right on the edge here,' said Mummy. 'This bed has only got edges.'

There was more loud crunching and squeaking as Daddy heaved himself out of the bed and across the room to the light switch.

Jeremy James sat up to get a good view of the remarkable bed.

'You certainly are on the edge,' said Daddy to Mummy. 'You must have moved.'

'I haven't moved,' said Mummy. 'It's what my mother used to call an M-bed.'

'An M-bed?' said Daddy.

'It sags in the middle,' said Mummy.

'Can I try it?' asked Jeremy James.

'Be our guest,' said Daddy.

Jeremy James climbed into the bed, which said kerdoing to him, too, and although he thought he was on the edge, he found himself nestling up against Mummy.

'It's a bit like a slide,' said Jeremy James.

'More like a retired trampoline,' said Daddy. 'Now what are we going to do?'

'I'll sleep here,' said Jeremy James. 'It's fun.'

'It might be fun for you,' said Daddy, 'but where are *we* going to sleep?'

'You could sleep on the floor,' said Jeremy James.

'Thanks very much,' said Daddy.

'That's not a bad idea,' said Mummy. 'We could shift the bed over to the window, and put the mattress down here on the floor.'

'I see what you mean,' said Daddy.

'That's if the floor doesn't sag as well. Good idea, Jeremy James.'

Mummy and Jeremy James got out of the bed and helped Daddy to push it towards the window. It was a very heavy bed, and they could only move it an inch at a time, and with every movement it went bump, hump, creak and groan. The noise must have woken Christopher, because he suddenly let out a piercing howl.

'Oh dear,' said Mummy, and stopped pushing the bed so that she could pick Christopher up. 'Jeremy James,' she said, 'could you just sit in the chair and hold Christopher, while Daddy and I finish moving the bed?'

Jeremy James sat down in the armchair, which also said kerdoing, and Mummy carefully placed Christopher in his arms. 'Wah, wah!' said Christopher, kerdoing said the armchair, and bump-hump-creak-groan said the bed, as Mummy and Daddy continued pushing it towards the window.

In the middle of all this loud activity, there was a knock at the door.

'Was that the door?' said Daddy.

'No,' said Jeremy James, 'I think it was somebody knocking at the door.'

Daddy went to the door and opened it. And there in the doorway stood a man in a red dressing gown. The man had a bald head and a twiddly moustache, and an angry expression in between.

'What the devil do you think you're up to?' said the man. 'We can't get any sleep at all.'

'Nor can we,' said Daddy. 'I'm terribly sorry, but we're trying to arrange things so that we *can* get some sleep.'

'Arrange things?' said the man. 'Sounds as if you're moving house! All that banging and crashing.'

33

'Well, we're shifting the bed so that we can put the mattress down on the floor,' said Daddy. 'The bed sags in the middle, you see, and...'

'Oh,' said the man with the twiddly moustache, 'now that's a good idea. Our bed sags as well.'

'It was Jeremy James who thought of it,' said Daddy.

'Clever lad,' said the man. 'I've fallen out of bed twice already. Here, let me give you a hand with that thing.'

And so saying, the man came into the room and helped Mummy and Daddy push the bed across to the window. It still went with a bump and a groan, but it went a lot quicker.

'There, that should do it,' said the man. 'Weigh a ton, these old beds. Pity they didn't make the middle as solid as the ends, eh?'

'Thanks very much for your help,' said Daddy. 'Can I come and do the same for you?'

'That's all right, I'll manage. Damn good idea that. We've been here three days and I haven't had a wink. Good night to you.'

And off he went. Daddy relieved Jeremy James of Christopher, who was quiet now, and Mummy got the bed ready on the floor.

'Fancy sticking this for three days!' said Daddy. 'No wonder Mrs Gullick likes to be paid in advance.'

When the bed was ready, and Christopher was back in the pram-top, and Jeremy James was snug and cosy, and Mummy was curled up on the mattress, Daddy turned out the light.

'Ah, that's better!' said Daddy, as he slid between the covers with no creaks except from his knees. 'Peace and quiet at last.'

And just then there was a loud bumping and humping from down below.

'Ah,' said Daddy, 'that'll be the moustache following our example.'

'I expect everyone'll be shifting beds soon,' said Mummy. 'Maybe by breakfast time, we shall all be asleep.'

A loud voice came from down below: 'Will you stop that infernal noise! There's people trying to sleep!'

And then Jeremy James heard the

35

voice of the man with the twiddly moustache: 'Awfully sorry. We're shifting the bed so we can put the mattress on the floor.'

'Mattress on the floor?' said the first voice.

'So we can get some sleep!' said the twiddly moustache.

'I say,' said the first voice. 'That's a good idea.'

'Little boy upstairs thought of it,' said the twiddly moustache.

After that there was a good deal more banging and creaking from down below, and Jeremy James heard more voices, though they weren't so distinct. But by now he was so tired that he couldn't really be bothered to listen to what they were saying. The last thing he heard was Mummy and Daddy laughing from the floor, and the last thing he thought was what fun it was to be on holiday. And then he went off into a lovely deep sleep.

CHAPTER FOUR

THE LOST ONES

It was very early in the morning when Jeremy James crept down the dark, creaky stairs of Mrs Gullick's house. Up in the attic, Mummy and Daddy were fast asleep, phwee-phewing and grrr-hoik-rumbling from their mattress on the floor, while the twins lay quietly in their pram-top. Jeremy James had been awake for hours, and he had been thinking about Mrs Gullick and her lost husband and son. He knew from experience that losing things can be a very upsetting business. He was always losing sweets and bits of chocolate. Mummy said he lost them down in his tummy, but even if you lost things in your tummy, it still meant you hadn't got them any more.

Once Mummy and Daddy had thought they'd lost Jeremy James. They'd gone out for the evening, and Jeremy James had played hide-and-seek with the babysitter. He'd been so good at hiding, while the babysitter was so bad at seeking, that the babysitter had sent for the police. Of course, Jeremy James hadn't been lost at all, because he knew just where he was. Fast asleep in Daddy's tool shed. But Mummy and Daddy had *thought* he was lost, and they'd certainly been unhappy. So it must be much worse for Mrs Gullick, because not even Jeremy James knew where her husband and son were. And so Jeremy James had decided to try and find them, and that was why he was creeping down Mrs Gullick's stairs.

At the foot of the stairs was a door, and although it seemed unlikely that Mr Gullick and James would hide in such an obvious place, Jeremy James opened the door just to make sure.

'What the devil ...?' said a vaguely familiar voice.

Jeremy James looked around, looked up, and then looked down, and there on the floor was a shiny head and a twiddly moustache poking out from under a blanket.

'Oh it's you,' said the man. 'You've

come to the wrong room, sonny.'

Next to the shiny head and twiddly moustache was a head that was covered with curlers and an expression of wide-eyed surprise. Jeremy James decided that neither of these heads belonged to the Gullicks, and he quickly closed the door.

'In any case,' said Jeremy James to himself, 'Mrs Gullick would have looked in all the doors you can see. It's no good looking in doors you can see. I'll have to find a door you can't see.'

Jeremy James walked slowly along the passage, ignoring all the doors he could see, and looking hard for a door which he couldn't see. But he didn't see one. The only interesting thing he did see was a pair of shoes standing in front of one of

the ordinary seeable doors. They were nice shoes, black and shiny, and whoever had lost them would obviously be very upset at losing them. Jeremy James decided that it would be helpful if he could place the shoes where the person might find them most easily. He thought hard for a moment.

'The only place where everybody has to go,' said Jeremy James to himself, 'is the front door. So if I put them outside the front door, the man is sure to find them.'

Jeremy James picked up the shoes and carried them all the way down to the ground floor. Then he walked along the passage to the front door, opened it, and put the shoes on the step outside.

'He can't miss them there,' said Jeremy James. 'And I'll bet he'll be pleased to find them.'

When Jeremy James closed the front door and turned round, he suddenly noticed a curtain in the hall. It was a dark curtain that covered the back of the stairs, and if it hadn't been for a shaft of sunlight falling on it, he probably wouldn't have noticed it at all.

'I wonder,' said Jeremy James, 'I just wonder if ... perhaps ... there might just possibly ...'

Slowly he pulled the bottom of the curtain to one side. And behind the curtain, completely hidden from sight, was a door. Even Mrs Gullick could never have spotted that door behind the curtain. It was the sort of door you would only see if you were looking for a door that *nobody* could see.

'That's where they are,' said Jeremy James. 'No wonder Mrs Gullick couldn't find them.'

He pulled the curtain again to reveal the door handle, reached up, and turned it. The door didn't open. He tugged hard. The door yielded a little, but something seemed to be holding it closed.

'Maybe Mr Gullick is pulling it the other way,' thought Jeremy James. 'Because he doesn't want to be found.'

Jeremy James took a deep breath, puffed out his chest like a pigeon, and gave the door an almighty heave. It flew open, and Jeremy James lost his grip and fell hard on his bottom. When he picked himself up, he found himself confronted not by Mr Gullick, but by a flight of stone steps that led downwards into very uninviting, very ghostly, very dead-body darkness. Jeremy James stood on the top step and peered down.

'Mr Gullick,' he called softly. 'I can see you!'

But Mr Gullick remained unseen.

'I've found you!' said Jeremy James.

But Mr Gullick remained unfound.

Then Jeremy James noticed a light switch on the wall by the door. Perhaps Mr Gullick had switched it off so that he wouldn't be seen. Jeremy James smiled, and switched it on.

'I'm coming,' he said. 'Here I come, Mr Gullick.'

Slowly and carefully he eased his way down the steep stone steps, holding tightly to the rail at the side. At the bottom he found himself in a huge, gloomy room lit only by a single bulb, which seemed to throw more shadows than it did light. Jeremy James stood quite still, until his eyes had grown accustomed to the gloom, and then he started to go forward in order to

investigate all the interesting objects that lay scattered over the floor. But at that very moment there was a loud *crash* at the top of the steps, and Jeremy James was so startled that his body almost jumped off his legs.

When Jeremy James had put himself together again, he looked up, and to his horror he saw that the door was tightly closed. He scrambled up the steps as fast as he could, turned the handle, and pushed. But the door wouldn't open. He banged on it with his fists, he kicked it, he bumped it with his bottom, he charged it with his shoulder, he shouted 'Help!' at the top of his voice ... but still the door remained tightly closed. Maybe this was what had happened to Mr Gullick and James: they had hidden down here, the door had gone crash, and they'd never been found again.

Jeremy James sat on the top step. His eyes were stinging, and the sting soon changed itself into tears that went rolling down his cheeks and plopping on to the second step. Mummy and Daddy would wake up and see that he wasn't in his bed. They'd hunt in all the cupboards and all the boxes and all the beds. They'd hunt in the bathroom, the bedrooms, the garden, the tool shed. But nobody would ever dream of pulling aside the dark curtain behind the stairs. Not even the police would think of that. And after a while, Mummy and Daddy would load the twins into the car and drive slowly and sadly away from Warkin-on-Sea, and they'd tell everybody they'd been to the seaside and lost Jeremy James. The thought was too terrible to think, and the tears plopped faster and faster on to the second step.

But heroes don't get out of difficult situations by sitting on steps and crying. And so after a while Jeremy James wiped his eyes on his pyjama sleeve, tightened up his lips, and asked himself: What would Daddy do? Well, Daddy would think about it, and then ... he'd ask Mummy what to do. So what would Mummy do? Mummy would say: 'Don't be silly, of course you can open the door.'

So Jeremy James banged, kicked, bumped, charged and shouted again. But the door wouldn't open.

'I can't,' he said. 'It won't move.'

So now what would Mummy do? She'd probably say: 'Let's have a cup of tea.' Only that was no good either. What had Mummy said the other day when those silly jigsaw pieces had refused to go in? 'If they won't go in one way, try them another way.' And they *had* gone in, too. 'If you can't go out one way,' Mummy would say, 'try another way.'

Jeremy James went down the steps with a determined look on his face. There must be another door or a window somewhere. He walked slowly all round the walls. No doors, no windows. He looked up at the ceiling. No doors or windows there either. He looked at the floor. Nothing but piles of boxes and ... was that a rocking horse? Jeremy James went nearer. Yes, it was. Rather different from his rocking horse at home, this one was big and clumsy and covered with dust, but ... Jeremy James got on and, yes, it rocked very well, even though it squeaked and groaned rather like the kerdoinging bed. And what was that over there? Jeremy James dismounted, and inspected the next object. It was a

46

pram—a very old pram with dusty hood and rusty wheels.

'That's James Gullick's pram,' said Jeremy James, 'and James Gullick's rocking horse. I wonder why he keeps them down here?'

Next to the pram was an old cot, and in the cot was a teddy bear with one ear. It wasn't a soft cuddly teddy bear, but was hard and patchy.

'Your toys are a bit funny,' said Jeremy James. 'My Mummy and Daddy give me much nicer things to play with.'

Jeremy James looked inside some of the boxes, and they were also full of old things—lamp-shades, books, newspapers, clothes, paintings. One nice wooden box looked as if it might contain a treasure, but when Jeremy James opened it, all he found was some bundles of letters tied up in ribbons. Some of the boxes had cobwebs on them, and when a big spider danced across Jeremy James's finger, he decided the boxes were not worth looking into anyway. And he started getting nasty tickly feelings all down his spine and over his face.

'I wish I could find a way out of here,' he said, and his eyes began to sting again.

*   *   *

Meanwhile, there was a great deal of activity in the house. Mummy was trying to cope with a pair of hungry twins, Daddy was knocking on people's doors and asking whether anyone had seen Jeremy James, the man with the twiddly moustache was trying to fix up his bed, which had collapsed last night when he had moved it across to the window, and a short man with monocle and a grey suit was walking barefoot up and down the passage looking for his shoes. The man with the twiddly moustache told Daddy about Jeremy James's visit, but the man with the monocle hadn't seen any little boys, and in any case he wasn't interested in little boys, he was interested in his shoes. Daddy and the man with the twiddly moustache walked up and down shouting 'Jeremy James!' and the man with the monocle walked down and up shouting 'Where are my shoes?' and some other people poked their heads out of their doors and shouted 'What's the matter?'

A short time before, Mrs Gullick had collected her newspaper from the front door, noticed that the cellar door was open, and so closed it. Now she left off preparing the breakfasts in order to investigate the disturbance.

'What,' said Mrs Gullick, 'is the meaning of this shouting?'

'Ah, Mrs Gullick,' said Daddy. 'You haven't seen Jeremy James, have you?'

'No, I haven't,' said Mrs Gullick.

'Ah, Mrs Gullick,' said a voice further up the stairs. 'You haven't seen my shoes, have you?'

'No,' said Mrs Gullick, 'I haven't.'

'Did you clean them?' said the voice, which was soon followed by the man with the monocle.

'No,' said Mrs Gullick, 'I didn't.'

'But I left them outside my door,' said the man with the monocle.

'Then outside your door,' said Mrs Gullick, 'is where they should be.'

'Well they're not,' said the man with the monocle.

'Then they must be somewhere else,'

said Mrs Gullick.

'Mrs Gullick,' said Daddy, 'are you sure you haven't seen Jeremy James?'

'No, I haven't,' said Mrs Gullick. 'Wasn't he with you last night?'

'Of course he was,' said Daddy. 'But when we woke up this morning, he was gone.'

'So were my shoes,' said the man with the monocle.

'Perhaps,' said the man with the twiddly moustache, 'your Jeremy James has walked off with this gentleman's shoes.'

'My Jeremy James,' said Daddy, 'would never walk off anywhere without having his breakfast. Could he have got himself locked in anywhere, Mrs Gullick?'

A thought came into Mrs Gullick's head. She had wondered at the time, but had assumed that the wind had blown the door open.

'Just a moment,' she said.

Daddy, the man with the twiddly moustache, and the barefooted man with the monocle followed Mrs Gullick along the hall to the back of the stairs.

Mrs Gullick pulled aside the curtain, and tugged open the cellar door.

'Jeremy James, are you down there?' she called.

'Yes I am, yes I am!' came the voice of Jeremy James. 'Don't close the door!' And he came racing up the stone steps, out of the door, and into Daddy's arms.

'What on earth were you doing down there?' asked Daddy, lifting him up high and holding him very tight.

'I was looking for Mr Gullick and James,' said Jeremy James.

'Oh, good heavens!' said Mrs Gullick. 'But they're both dead, Jeremy James.'

'Dead?' said Jeremy James. 'But you said you'd lost them.'

'Lost,' said Daddy, 'is just a way people have of saying that someone is dead. I'm ever so sorry, Mrs Gullick.'

Mrs Gullick dabbed her eyes. 'What a dear, sweet boy,' she said, and hurried off to the breakfast room to have a little cry.

'I suppose,' said the man with the monocle, 'your little boy doesn't happen to have seen my shoes, does he?'

'You haven't seen a pair of shoes wandering around, have you, Jeremy James?' asked Daddy.

'Black shoes?' asked Jeremy James. 'Shiny black shoes?'

'That's right,' said the man with the monocle. 'I left them outside my bedroom door.'

'Oh, I thought they were lost,' said Jeremy James. 'Or rather, dead. I put them outside the front door so you'd find them.'

The man with the monocle went to the front door, opened it, and stepped gingerly outside.

'Come on, Jeremy James,' said Daddy. 'I think Mummy's waiting for us upstairs.'

He winked at the man with the twiddly moustache, and they set off up the stairs at top speed, with Jeremy James jogging up and down on Daddy's shoulder.

'This is much better than James's old rocking horse,' said Jeremy James.

'I don't know about James's old rocking horse,' said Daddy. 'But it's certainly better than a shiny black shoe on your bottom.'

CHAPTER FIVE

CASTLES IN THE SAND

Jeremy James was sorry to leave Mrs Gullick's, and Mrs Gullick was sorry to say goodbye to Jeremy James. But she gave him a large bar of chocolate 'for the journey', and this helped greatly to sweeten the parting.

When they were out of sight from Mrs Gullick's, Daddy set off to look for another hotel, while Mummy and Jeremy James pushed the twins' pram in the direction of the beach. On the way they stopped to buy a bucket and spade, and Jeremy James put the spade over his shoulder and oompah-oompahed down to the golden sands of Warkin-on-Sea. And as his feet sank into the soft carpet, it was like stepping into another world. The first men to step on the moon couldn't have been more excited than Jeremy James stepping on to the beach at Warkin-on-Sea. Mummy spread a large blanket over the sand and then helped

Jeremy James into his bathing costume, and he gazed wide-eyed all round him. There were lots of people on the beach: all ages and colours and shapes and sizes. Near by lay a man with a huge tummy.

'Oh Mummy,' said Jeremy James, 'do you think he's got twins in his tummy?'

'Sh!' said Mummy. 'Don't talk so loud! Of course he hasn't. Men don't have babies.'

'But isn't he fat!' cried Jeremy James.

'Sh, Jeremy James!' said Mummy. 'He'll hear you.'

'No he won't,' said Jeremy James. 'He's asleep.'

At that moment the fat man waved away a fly that had mistaken his stomach

for a giant slide.

'Anyway,' whispered Jeremy James, 'I expect he knows he's fat. He'd have to be silly not to know he's fat.'

'Yes, all right, Jeremy James,' said Mummy, 'just don't shout about it.'

'Where's the sea gone, Mummy?' asked Jeremy James.

'It's gone out,' said Mummy. 'It's what's called low tide. It goes out and then comes in again.'

'You mean like Daddy when he's doing the gardening?' asked Jeremy James.

'Something like that,' said Mummy with a smile.

'What are those red flags for out there?' asked Jeremy James.

'They're to warn people not to go any further,' said Mummy. 'Nobody must go beyond those flags.'

'Why, Mummy?' asked Jeremy James.

'Because it's dangerous,' said Mummy.

'Why is it dangerous?' asked Jeremy James.

'Because you can get caught by the tide,' said Mummy.

'How can you get caught by the tide?' asked Jeremy James, but Mummy had had enough of the questions, and shooed Jeremy James off to go and build sandcastles while she stretched out on the blanket with the twins.

Jeremy James wandered off with his bucket and spade until he found a good spot that nobody had dug up, pressed down, or sat on. And here he set out to break the world record for brilliant sandcastle building. He began to dig a large, circular moat, and although the circle gradually became less and less round and more and more square with sudden diversions, Jeremy James felt he was doing well. And then suddenly a familiar voice said:

'That's not a very good moat.'

Jeremy James looked up from his digging, and there stood a ginger-haired, freckle-faced boy with a very superior expression on his face. His name was Timothy Smyth-Fortescue, and he lived in the big house next door to Jeremy James's. Timothy Smyth-Fortescue had everything, did everything, and knew everything.

'It's all over the place,' said Timothy. 'Moats should be round, not all over the place.'

'I'll bet you couldn't dig a better one,' said Jeremy James.

'Oh yes I could,' said Timothy. 'That's my castle over there, and it's miles better than yours.'

'I've only just started mine,' said Jeremy James.

'Well, your moat's all crooked,' said Timothy. 'Moats should be round, not crooked.'

'I didn't want a round moat,' said Jeremy James. 'I wanted mine to be crooked.'

'Why?' asked Timothy.

'Because,' said Jeremy James.

'Because what?' asked Timothy.

'Because...' said Jeremy James, 'because round moats are old-fashioned. My Daddy told me round moats are old-fashioned. People don't build round moats any more.'

'You're just saying that,' said Timothy, 'because you can't build a round moat. You don't know how to.'

'Oh yes I do,' said Jeremy James.

'Go on then,' said Timothy. 'Make a round moat.'

'I won't,' said Jeremy James.

'You can't,' said Timothy. 'You come and look at my castle, and then you'll see how proper castles are built.'

'Right,' said Jeremy James, with a determined look on his face. 'You show me your rotten castle. I'll bet it's a rotten castle. I'll bet your castle isn't nearly as good as my castle's going to be. 'Cos I'm going to build the best castle *anybody's ever* built.'

By now they had reached Timothy's castle. And it wasn't a rotten castle at all. It was a very good castle. In fact it was so good that it may well have been the best castle anybody had ever built. It had a completely round moat, lots of smooth regular towers, battlements, a drawbridge. It looked just like a real castle.

'There you are,' said Timothy. '*That's* how to build a sandcastle. And I'll bet *you* couldn't build a sandcastle like that.'

'It's all right,' said Jeremy James. 'But I've seen better ones.'

'Where?' demanded Timothy.

'Places,' said Jeremy James.
'What places?' demanded Timothy.
'Well,' said Jeremy James, 'places like
… like … the Grandmother Polly

Ann...'

'The what?' said Timothy.

'The Grandmother Polly Ann. It's a hotel...'

'You mean the Grand Metropolitan,' said Timothy. 'That's where I'm staying. And I haven't seen you there.'

'No,' said Jeremy James, 'because I'm not staying there, because we didn't want to stay there. *We've* been at Mrs Gullick's, so there.'

'The Grand Metropolitan's got five stars. I'll bet Mrs Gullick hasn't got five stars,' said Timothy.

'Who cares about stars?' said Jeremy James. 'I had two eggs and two slices of bacon for breakfast.'

'I had poached haddock,' said Timothy. 'And four slices of toast.'

'Mrs Gullick gave me a big bar of chocolate, too,' said Jeremy James.

'Chocolate's bad for your teeth,' said Timothy. 'You shouldn't eat chocolate.'

'And you shouldn't eat poach taddock,' said Jeremy James. 'Poach taddock makes people die.'

'No it doesn't,' said Timothy.

'Yes it does,' said Jeremy James. 'I

know somebody who died of poach taddock.'

'Who?' asked Timothy.

'My Mummy's Great-Aunt Maud. She ate poach taddock, and they had to put her in a box and throw her away.'

The conversation would doubtless have continued, but at this moment Timothy's mother, in a swimming costume and sunglasses, approached the sandcastle.

'Come along, Timothy,' she said, 'we're going back to the hotel now. Oh hello, Jeremy. Fancy seeing you here! Have you come with your mummy and daddy?'

'Yes, Mrs Smyth-Forseasick,' said Jeremy James, who always had some difficulty with Timothy's mother's name.

'Well, say hello to them for me, Jeremy,' said Mrs Smyth-Fortescue.

Jeremy James was about to remind her that his name was Jeremy *James* when she suddenly said something that he found very interesting indeed.

'What a beautiful sandcastle!' she said. 'That *is* good! Did you build that all by yourself, Jeremy?'

'No,' said Jeremy James, 'I didn't build it at all. Timothy built it.'

'Timothy,' said Mrs Smyth-Fortescue, 'did you tell Jeremy that *you* built it?'

Timothy's face went red, and he looked down at his right foot which was burying itself as deep as possible in the sand.

'You mustn't say things like that, dear,' said Mrs Smyth-Fortescue. 'It's very naughty to tell lies. Come along now, perhaps you can play with Jeremy again this afternoon. Say goodbye, dear.'

'G'bye,' said Timothy, still studying his right foot.

'G'bye,' said Jeremy James. 'Hope you have poach taddock for lunch.'

Off went Timothy with his mother, and Jeremy James returned to his crooked moat. Perhaps his sandcastle wouldn't be quite the best anybody had ever built, but at least it would be his. Jeremy James gave a cheerful smile, and began to dig.

CHAPTER SIX

THE DONKEY

Jeremy James had swung and trampolined, he had boated and merry-gone-round, and now he was all set for a donkey ride over the sands. There were twelve donkeys in all, and when Jeremy James and Daddy arrived, eleven of them already had riders. The twelfth had stuck his nose in a bucket of hay and was munching as happily as if it were a bucket of strawberries and cream. Daddy lifted Jeremy James up into the saddle, and gave some money to a young man who wore swimming trunks and a straw hat.

'Off we go then!' said Straw Hat. 'Come on, Speedy!' And he gave Jeremy James's donkey a slap.

Off went the young man, and off went eleven donkeys, but Jeremy James's donkey kept his feet in the sand and his nose in the bucket.

'He's not moving,' said Jeremy James.

Daddy gave Speedy a slap and cried: 'Off we go!' But off Speedy did not go.

'Oy!' shouted Daddy after the young man with the straw hat, but the young man simply strolled on, followed by eleven plodding donkeys with eleven contented riders. And the twelfth donkey munched his hay.

'I don't think he wants to go,' said Jeremy James.

'We've paid for a ride,' said Daddy, 'and a ride is what you shall have.'

Daddy pulled hard on the bridle, and went very red in the face, but Speedy didn't move.

'Having trouble?' asked a fat man with a wobbly tummy.

'Donkey won't go,' said Daddy. 'We

paid our money, and he refuses to move.'

'I'll give you a hand,' said the fat man.

Then Daddy pulled and the fat man pushed. They pulled and pushed till they were both puffing like steam engines, but Speedy stood as still as a rock.

'He doesn't want to go,' Jeremy James told the fat man. 'That's the trouble.'

'Don't keep saying that!' said Daddy. 'He's *got* to go. One more effort!'

Daddy pulled and the fat man pushed, and the donkey took one step forward and trod on Daddy's foot.

'Ow!' said Daddy, and let go of the bridle.

'Oof!' said the fat man, and fell on his tummy.

'Hee haw!' said Speedy, and returned to his bucket of hay.

'It's no good,' said the fat man, getting up from the sand. 'You'll have to wait till the owner comes back.'

'Looks like it,' said Daddy, sitting down in the sand and holding on to his foot. 'He just doesn't want to go, that's the trouble.'

Daddy waggled his foot, and the fat man wobbled away, and Jeremy James sat on Speedy wondering how he could persuade the donkey to move. Daddy had tried ordering, coaxing, pushing and pulling, but Daddy was never very good at getting things to go. Jeremy James remembered the car, the washing machine, the TV set, and even his railway set refusing to go when Daddy told them to. Daddy asking Speedy to move was just like Jeremy James asking Mummy for ice cream instead of potatoes—a waste of breath and time.

'If I was a donkey,' said Jeremy James to himself, 'I'd certainly stay still when Daddy told me to go. And that's a fact.'

But the donkey also stayed still when Jeremy James told him to go. And this gave Jeremy James an idea. If the donkey stayed still when he was told to go, what would he do if you told him to stand still?

Jeremy James leaned forward in the saddle, and whispered in Speedy's ear: 'Stay here, Speedy. Good boy. You stay here.'

Speedy raised his head from the bucket, gave a wheezy sort of grunt, and slowly trotted away.

Daddy scrambled to his one good

foot. 'Hey, come back!' he shouted.

This seemed a little strange to Jeremy James, as Daddy had just spent such a long time trying to get Speedy to move off. But it didn't matter anyway, because Speedy simply trotted a little faster.

'Go back!' cried Jeremy James, and Speedy went forward, as Daddy came limp-hobble-puffing after them.

Jeremy James looked down, and the sand became a golden blur beneath Speedy's pounding hooves. But they had to go faster still if they were not to be caught by the thousand Red Indians that were chasing them.

'Slow down!' shouted Jeremy James. 'Speedy, slow down!'

'Oh dear!' said a pretty girl in a red bathing costume. 'Look at that little boy. He wants the donkey to slow down, and it's going even faster!'

'I'll stop them!' said the young man who was sitting next to the pretty girl. 'You watch me!' And he stuck out his chest and ran in front of Speedy, waving his arms and shouting: 'Whoa!'

'Let him catch you,' whispered Jeremy James, and Speedy promptly swerved right round the young man, who lunged, missed, and fell flat on his face.

'Come back!' cried the young man, on his knees in the sand.

'Come back!' cried Daddy, falling even further behind.

'Go back!' cried Jeremy James, with a smile all over his face.

And Speedy sped on. Two boys playing football leapt out of his path, and a lady with a Pekinese dog said 'Good heavens!' as donkey and rider raced by. 'Wuff wuff!' said the Pekinese dog, and chased after Speedy. 'Come back, Montague!' shouted the lady, and chased after the Pekinese dog.

The sight of all these running figures attracted the attention of a brown dog and a black dog, and before long there was a trail of dogs, dog-owners, men, women and children, and—last of all—Daddy chasing Speedy and Jeremy James along the beach.

'Slow down!' cried Jeremy James, thoroughly enjoying himself, and Speedy ran faster and faster.

No doubt they would have ridden right off the sand, out of Warkin-on-Sea and as far as the Rocky Mountains if the young man with the straw hat had not caught hold of Speedy's bridle.

'Whoa there, Speedy!' he cried, and to Jeremy James's disappointment, Speedy

came to an abrupt halt. So too did the Pekinese dog, four other dogs, five dog-owners, six children, seven men and women, and—eventually—Daddy.

'I dunno what you been up to,' said Straw Hat. 'Gallopin' like a racehorse he was!'

'I haven't been up to anything,' said Jeremy James. 'He wouldn't go.'

'Wouldn't go?' said Straw Hat. 'Wouldn't go! He'd have won the Derby goin' like that!'

'It's not the boy's fault!' said a man with a black dog and a red face. 'You should keep your donkeys under control.'

'Hear, hear!' said the woman with the Pekinese. And 'Wuff wuff!' said the Pekinese.

'Are you all right, Jeremy James?' asked Daddy, panting through the crowd.

'Yes thank you,' said Jeremy James.

'He's a little hero,' said a woman. 'The way he stayed on that donkey! I'd have been terrified!'

Then several people in the crowd murmured: 'Hero ... very brave ... could

71

have been a disaster . . .'

Jeremy James smiled heroically as Daddy lifted him off the saddle and on to his shoulders.

'That donkey,' said Daddy to Straw Hat, 'is very dangerous. He nearly broke my foot, and he could easily have injured my son.'

People in the crowd mumbled: 'Dangerous . . . could have been killed . . . should be prosecuted . . . licence taken away . . .' and other long words that sounded threatening. Straw Hat looked very uncomfortable. Finally, he dipped his hand in the leather bag that hung from his shoulder, and pulled out a handful of coins.

'Sorry, mister,' he said. 'Perhaps you could buy your lad an ice cream to make up for it.'

Jeremy James smiled even more heroically.

'Can't understand it, though,' said Straw Hat. 'Speedy never bolted before. We call him "Speedy" as a joke, 'cos he's always so slow.'

The crowd dispersed, and Jeremy James rode Daddy back along the beach.

It was a slow, bumpy ride, not nearly as exciting as the gallop on Speedy. But when Jeremy James realized that it was in fact a limp towards the ice cream van, he began to enjoy the return journey almost as much as the first ride.

It was while he was unwrapping his Moon Rocket Lolly that Jeremy James happened to glance back up the beach again. There in the distance he could see the young man in the straw hat, and the young man was pulling hard at the bridle of a donkey that was obviously refusing to move.

'Looks like Speedy's got stuck again,' said Daddy.

'That,' said Jeremy James, 'is because Straw Hat's not saying the right thing to him.'

'Aha!' said Daddy. 'And what *is* the right thing?'

'The right thing,' said Jeremy James, licking his Moon Rocket, 'is the wrong thing.'

Daddy smiled. 'Well, I must remember that,' he said.

But Jeremy James knew Daddy didn't

really understand. Grown-ups are often very slow when it comes to understanding children. And donkeys.

CHAPTER SEVEN

TOTTY BOTTY

The new hotel had no creaking beds, no dark staircases, no mysterious cellars. It was very clean, very modern, and rather boring. It had a posh restaurant, though, and Jeremy James decided that it was time he varied his diet. He therefore chose chicken and chips, followed by strawberries and ice cream, and accompanied by Coca-Cola.

'I thought you were going to try something different,' said Daddy.

'I am,' said Jeremy James. 'I'm having chicken.'

'He usually has fish,' said Mummy.

The waiter, who had black hair, a black moustache and a black jacket, bent low over the table.

'Would sir lika da tomato ketchuppa widda chips?' he asked.

'Pardon?' said Jeremy James.

'Would you like tomato ketchup?' said Daddy.

75

'Oh, yes please,' said Jeremy James.

'Tell the waiter, then,' said Daddy.

The waiter was writing something down on a pad.

'Yes, please,' said Jeremy James, but

the waiter didn't seem to hear. Instead he finished writing, and then bent low again.

'Anda da lemon inna da Coca-Cola, ha?'

'Why doesn't he talk properly, Daddy?' asked Jeremy James.

'He's asking if you want lemon in your Coca-Cola,' said Daddy.

Jeremy James looked straight up at the waiter. 'You talk funny,' he said. The waiter looked straight down at Jeremy James. 'I no talka funny,' he said. 'You hear funny.'

Mummy and Daddy both laughed, and so did the waiter, but Jeremy James frowned.

'He's Italian,' whispered Mummy, when the waiter had gone. 'He doesn't come from this country. That's why he doesn't speak English properly.'

'Why doesn't anybody teach him?' whispered Jeremy James.

'I expect they've tried,' whispered Mummy. 'But English is a very difficult language.'

'Is it?' whispered Jeremy James. 'I don't think it is. I speak properly, and

I'm not nearly as old as he is.'

'Ah, but do you speak Italian?' asked Daddy.

'What's Italian?' asked Jeremy James.

'Hm,' said Daddy, 'how do you explain that?'

'Different people,' said Mummy, 'come from different countries, and so they speak different languages. Like we say "eat" and the French say "manger" and the Germans say ... what do the Germans say?'

'"Essen",' said Daddy. 'And the Italians say "mangiare". Different people have different words.'

'Well that's silly,' said Jeremy James. 'Why don't they have the same words? Then they wouldn't have to talk in a funny way.'

'You're right,' said Daddy. 'It would make life easier if everyone spoke the same language. But which language should everybody speak?'

'English,' said Jeremy James.

'But that,' said Daddy, 'would only make life easier for *us*.'

At that moment, an elderly man who was sitting at the next table leaned across

78

and grinned at Daddy.

'*Voilà l'Anglais typique!*' he said, pointing at Jeremy James.

Daddy laughed and said something else that Jeremy James couldn't understand, and then he and the other man started making all kinds of strange noises with their noses and throats.

'That's French,' whispered Mummy. 'Daddy and the man are speaking French.'

But the more Jeremy James listened, the less like speaking it seemed. The elderly man made his noises very fast, and sounded as if he was holding his nose, and Daddy occasionally made some noises of his own, though these were slower, and Jeremy James recognized one sound that he knew, which was "er". But even Daddy wasn't using proper words, and although he and the elderly man laughed as if they understood each other, Jeremy James knew that this must be some silly game.

All through the meal Jeremy James was unusually quiet. When Mummy asked him if his chicken was all right, he simply grunted, and when Daddy asked him if he was full, he merely nodded. And when the waiter said: 'Issa good, no?' he looked up and said 'Mhm, mhm!'

It was only when they were back in the hotel bedroom (where the twins were already asleep) that Jeremy James began to talk in words again. Mummy said to him:

'Bedtime now, so get your pyjamas on.'

And Jeremy James said: 'Cobbly wobbly chucka-bung bung.'

'Pardon?' said Mummy.

'Wobble wabble doople dums,' said Jeremy James. 'And socky dock.'

'Good heavens!' said Daddy. 'Our son's speaking a foreign language!'

'Dabble gabble,' said Jeremy James. 'Umbly totty botty.'

'Aha,' said Mummy, 'now I wonder what language it is.'

'It's certainly not English,' said Daddy. 'And it doesn't look as if he understands English either. Do you understand English, Jeremy James?'

'Totty botty,' said Jeremy James.

'Totty botty,' said Daddy. 'No, I don't recognize that language at all. Listen,

Jeremy James, if you understand me, nod your head. And if you don't, then shake your head.'

Jeremy James shook his head.

'Aha,' said Daddy, 'caught you there. If you didn't understand, how did you know you should shake your head?'

'Soppy loppy maddy Daddy,' said Jeremy James.

'And totty botty to you,' said Daddy.

'If he doesn't get himself undressed for bed,' said Mummy, 'I shall give him a smack on his totty botty.'

Daddy knelt down in front of Jeremy James and looked at him very seriously.

'Clothes,' said Daddy, waving his arms, 'offy toffy. Pyjamas, onny ponny. And then ready steady beddy.'

Jeremy James gazed straight back into Daddy's eyes.

'Silly billy,' he said.

'And silly billy to you, too,' said Daddy. 'Now if Jeremy James gets his clothes offy woffy and his pyjamas onny wonny and dives straight into beddy weddy before Daddy counts up to one hundred, Jeremy James will have some more ice creamy dreamy in the morning.'

With a sudden flurry of activity, Jeremy James began to undress at world record undressing speed. Daddy stood up, and winked at Mummy.

'The trouble with you English,' he said, 'is that you never bother to learn other people's languages. Isn't that right, Jeremy James?'

Jeremy James nodded.

'But I'll tell you one thing, Jeremy James,' said Daddy. 'You'd better learn some English by the morning. Or you won't know what type of ice cream to ask for.'

'Issa good,' said Jeremy James. 'I speaka da English good.'

Mummy let out such a shriek of laughter that it woke Christopher up, and Christopher howled a howl which would have been understood in any language. But he didn't understand at all when Daddy told him to quieten down, and it was only when Mummy had picked him up and rocked him in her arms that he finally got the message.

'He no speaka da English,' said Daddy to Jeremy James.

'He too young,' said Jeremy James. 'Gotta da lot to learn.'

CHAPTER EIGHT

THE CASTLE TREASURE

'Are we doing anything special today?' asked Jeremy James.

'We're going to Warkin Castle,' said Mummy, putting an arrow-straight parting in Jeremy James's hair.

'A castle!' said Jeremy James. 'A real castle? With a moat and a drawbridge and dungeons and...'

'I expect so,' said Mummy.

'And things to torture people with?' asked Jeremy James.

'Like blunt razor blades,' said Daddy, dabbing his chin with a piece of cotton wool.

'I expect they've got everything there,' said Mummy, 'including sharp spikes for people like Daddy who can't get up in the morning.'

'Well, I had a shocking night,' said Daddy. 'All those car doors slamming. Slept better at Mrs Gullick's.'

'Can we go back to Mrs Gullick's

84

then?' asked Jeremy James.

'No,' said Daddy. 'I like to suffer in comfort.'

Eventually Daddy had finished yawning, rubbing his eyes, and dabbing his chin, and the family set off for Warkin Castle. Jeremy James kept a look-out for horses and knights in armour, but apart from the donkeys on the sand and the padded cricketers in the park, there was nothing much to see in the way of horses or knights.

Nor, as it turned out, was there very much in the way of castles. Warkin Castle had no moat, no drawbridge, no dungeons, no instruments of torture, no battlements, no roof ... in fact, the

harder Jeremy James looked, the less castle he could see. There were a few bits of wall scattered over the top of the hill, and there were piles of stones which looked as if they might be good for climbing, but the rest of Warkin Castle consisted of green grass and blue sky.

'Shall I buy a guidebook?' asked Daddy, as they waited at the ticket office.

'May as well,' said Mummy. 'Then we'll know what we're not seeing.'

'Do we have to pay to go in?' whispered Jeremy James to Mummy.

'Afraid so,' said Mummy.

Jeremy James frowned. This was a terrible waste of good money. Perhaps Mummy and Daddy hadn't realized that there wasn't any castle. Grown-ups often do miss things that children see straight away. More than once Jeremy James had spotted an ice cream van while Mummy and Daddy were looking quite the wrong way, and it was surprising how frequently they failed to notice interesting things like toy shops and cafés and playgrounds.

'Mummy,' he said, tugging at her

dress. 'You shouldn't pay. They've taken the castle away.'

But it was too late. Daddy had bought the tickets and the guidebook.

'Jeremy James says we shouldn't have paid,' Mummy told Daddy. 'Because they've taken the castle away.'

Daddy laughed. 'Quite right,' he said. 'It must be run by the government. You always have to pay them for things they take away.'

'Anyway,' Mummy said to Jeremy James, 'it's what's called a ruined castle. There *used* to be a castle here.'

'I don't think you should have to pay for something that *used* to be here,' said Jeremy James. 'I'd sooner pay for an ice cream that *is* here than a castle that isn't.'

They walked across the grass, with the twins bumping up and down in their pram, and Jeremy James looked scornfully round at the bits of wall and piles of stones. Daddy raised his nose from the guidebook and announced that they were now passing through the great gate.

'Doesn't look much like a gate to me,' grumbled Jeremy James. 'It's just a pile of stones.'

'Ah no, wait a minute,' said Daddy. 'My mistake. The great gate was back at the ticket office. Ugh, this is just a pile of stones. Let's see . . .'

Daddy seemed to have some difficulty in reading the guidebook, because every so often he would turn it sideways or backwards or upside-down, wave his arm around, and mumble things like: 'Kitchen . . . over there . . . or is it there . . . worple worple . . . blooming diagram . . .'

He did manage to work out that the castle had been built in the fifteenth century, which made it over five hundred years old, but as Jeremy James said, there wasn't anything clever in being over five hundred years old if you weren't there any more.

The only interesting item Daddy found in the guidebook was the fact that a treasure was supposed to lie buried somewhere in the castle, but it seemed to Jeremy James that as there was no castle left, it was highly unlikely that there would be any treasure left either. However, when Mummy and Daddy sat down on a bench with the twins, he decided he might just as well hunt for treasure as sit looking at grass and sky. At least it would be a good excuse for climbing on the walls.

'Stay where we can see you,' said Mummy. 'And don't go climbing on the walls.'

A look of great pain crossed Jeremy James's face. 'Well, can I just *look* at the walls?' he asked.

'Keep right away from them,' said Mummy. 'Those walls are dangerous.'

As walls didn't move, didn't scratch and didn't bite, Jeremy James asked how they could possibly be dangerous. Daddy pointed to a pile of stones and explained that once that pile had also been a wall, and he wouldn't like Jeremy James to be underneath when a wall decided to change into a pile of stones.

'So keep away from the walls,' he said, 'if *you* don't want to become a buried treasure.'

'But they're bound to have put the treasure in the walls!' said Jeremy James.

'People bury treasure in the ground,' said Daddy, 'If it's not in the ground, it won't be anywhere.'

Jeremy James had once found a treasure buried in the back garden. It hadn't been quite what he'd expected, because when he'd finally managed to break it open with a pickaxe, nothing had come out except a shower of water, and Mummy and Daddy hadn't been very pleased. But it proved that Daddy was probably right, and the ground *was* where people buried their treasure.

Jeremy James wandered over the hill. His mind went back to Mrs Gullick's secret door behind the curtain. Perhaps on the hill there was a patch of grass that wasn't grass at all, but a curtain hiding a secret door that would lead down into the treasure chamber. Jeremy James kept his eyes firmly fixed on the ground as he walked, and . . .

Bump!

'Where are you going, young man?' asked a crackly voice from high above the waistcoat that Jeremy James had bumped into.

Jeremy James looked up past a white beard and into a pair of twinkling blue eyes.

'Sorry!' said Jeremy James. 'I didn't

90

see you.'

'That's all right,' said the man with the white beard. 'I didn't see you either. Are you enjoying yourself then?'

'No,' said Jeremy James.

'Oh,' said the man with the white beard. 'Why not?'

'Because it's boring,' said Jeremy James. 'Castles should have moats and dungeons and torture things—not just piles of stones.'

'Well, it used to have them,' said the man, 'but then it got old and lost them all. The same thing happens to people.'

'People don't have moats and dungeons,' said Jeremy James.

'That's true,' said the man.

'And I was looking for a treasure,' said Jeremy James, 'but I expect the castle's lost that too.'

'Treasure, eh?' said the man.

'Yes,' said Jeremy James. 'It's supposed to be buried in the ground, but I can't find it.'

'Well, you keep searching,' said the man. 'You have to be patient to find buried treasure. But have a quick look up every now and then, just to see where you're going.'

The man with the white beard smiled, and Jeremy James fixed his eyes on the ground and resumed his search. But the grass and weeds and stones were as empty of treasure as the hill was empty of castle. He was just about to give up and go back to Mummy and Daddy when he heard the crackly voice again.

'I say, young man! Over here! Come and look over here!'

The man with the white beard was standing in some high weeds that came almost up to his knees, and he was waving his arm. Jeremy James ran across to him.

'Now I'm not quite sure,' said the man, 'but I've got a funny feeling that if you look very closely in here, you'll find some treasure. You'll have to look hard, mind.'

Then he chuckled and walked away. Jeremy James bent down and looked very hard amongst the weeds. He stepped forward a pace, then another pace, and ... just where the man had been standing, wedged under a small stone, was the unmistakable silver glint of a fifty pence piece.

Jeremy James picked it up and rushed back to Mummy and Daddy.

'Look what I found!' he cried. 'It's

treasure!'

'Where did you get it?' asked Mummy.

'Over there in the weeds!' said Jeremy James. 'The man with the white beard told me where it was. Look, there he is!'

Jeremy James waved, and in the distance the man with the white beard waved back. Then he disappeared behind a wall.

'There are some nice people around,' said Mummy.

'But I wonder how he knew it was there,' said Jeremy James.

'Perhaps he knows a lot about treasure-hunting,' said Daddy.

'And about treasure-hunters,' said Mummy with a smile.

CHAPTER NINE

THE RED FLAG

The family were down on the beach. Mummy was in her bathing costume, basking with the twins, and Daddy was gradually shedding his raincoat, jacket, pullover and shirt as the hot sun defied the weather forecasters, who had announced that there would be rain today.

Jeremy James picked up his bucket and spade, and went off to build a castle. This would be a real castle not a ruined castle, and it would be surrounded by a deep round moat that would be deeper and rounder than any moat had ever been before. He carefully selected a stretch of smooth level sand, and began to dig.

'You have to build the castle first,' said a familiar voice. 'You don't dig a moat before you've built the castle. Everyone knows that.'

'You don't know anything about

sandcastles,' said Jeremy James.

'Oh yes I do,' said Timothy. 'I've built hundreds of sandcastles.'

'You didn't build the sandcastle the other day,' said Jeremy James.

'I've built thousands of better castles than that,' said Timothy.

'Let's see them,' said Jeremy James.

'You can't see them now,' said Timothy. 'They all get squashed by the sea. You don't know anything.'

'Oh yes I do,' said Jeremy James. 'I know lots of things that you don't know.'

'Such as?' said Timothy.

'Such as...' said Jeremy James, 'such as... I know how old Warkin Castle is.'

'500 years old,' said Timothy. 'I've been there. It's all ruined.'

'You don't know what Italian is,' said Jeremy James.

'Oh yes I do,' said Timothy, 'because I've *been* to Italy. I've heard Italian people speaking Italian, so there.'

'Well, I'll bet you don't know what those red flags along the beach are for,' said Jeremy James.

'They're not for anything,' said

Timothy. 'They're just flags.'

'They are for something,' said Jeremy James, 'and you don't know what.'

'They're for decoration,' said Timothy. 'To make the place look cheerful. Everyone knows that.'

'You're wrong,' said Jeremy James, 'and you don't know everything, so there.'

'Well what are they for, then, clever?' asked Timothy.

'They're to stop the tide from catching you,' said Jeremy James.

Timothy's nose, which had been dipping in the direction of his toes, now suddenly rose in the air so that he could look down it again.

'The tide couldn't catch me,' he said. 'I can run faster than the tide. I don't need any old red flags to stop the tide from catching me. Anyway, flags can't stop anything. Flags can't move, can they? That's all silly talk.'

'You mustn't go beyond the flags,' said Jeremy James.

'Course you can,' said Timothy. 'Come on, I'll show you.'

'No, you're not supposed to,' said

Jeremy James.

'You're scared,' said Timothy. 'I'll race you there. I bet I can run faster than you.'

'No you can't,' said Jeremy James.

'Yes I can,' said Timothy.

And so the two of them raced over the sand, with their legs whirling and their faces twisted in determination. About halfway there, Jeremy James knew he'd won. Timothy wasn't even in the corner of his eye, and there was no sound of thudding footsteps in pursuit. But Jeremy James simply drove himself harder, and didn't stop until he had reached the red flag. Then puffing and snorting, rather like a sleeping Daddy, he turned to look for Timothy. There was no sign of him.

'That showed him,' said Jeremy James. 'I'm the world champion.'

'I'm over here,' came a voice from somewhere along the beach. 'And I won.'

Jeremy James looked round. Level with him, quite a way along the sand, stood another red flag, and beneath the other red flag stood Timothy, waving his arm and shouting: 'I won! I won!'

'No you didn't!' shouted Jeremy
James.

'Yes I did!' shouted Timothy. 'You
went to the wrong flag!'

'*You* went to the wrong flag!' shouted
Jeremy James. 'And you're a rotten
cheat!'

'Come over here,' shouted Timothy. 'I
want to show you something.'

Jeremy James didn't feel like going
over there. Jeremy James didn't feel like
being with Timothy at all. Timothy
couldn't possibly show Jeremy James
anything that Jeremy James would want
to see.

'Come on!' shouted Timothy.

'I won't!' shouted Jeremy James.

'All right, don't!' shouted Timothy.
'You'll be sorry! I don't care!'

Jeremy James decided he'd better go
and see what it was. He could always run
away afterwards.

'Look!' said Timothy, stretching out
his foot.

'What?' asked Jeremy James, who
couldn't see anything.

'My foot,' said Timothy.

'What about your silly foot?' asked Jeremy James.

'It's on the other side of the red flag,' said Timothy. 'And I haven't been caught by the tide, have I?'

Jeremy James looked more closely at the foot. It *was* on the other side of the flag, and a little trickle of water was just passing over it.

'Anyway,' said Jeremy James, 'most of you is on this side of the flag. You won't be caught if you're on this side of the flag.'

'You don't know anything,' said Timothy. 'I could go miles past the flag and the tide still couldn't catch me.'

'My Mummy says it's dangerous.'

'I bet your Mummy doesn't know anything either. Grown-ups just say things like that to frighten children like you. I could go right out there to the sky, and the tide wouldn't catch me.'

'No you couldn't,' said Jeremy James. 'You'd get lost.'

'How could you get lost in the sea!' sneered Timothy. 'It's just water. There's no streets in the sea.'

'Getting lost,' said Jeremy James, 'is just a way people have of saying getting dead. Don't you know that? You'd be dead, so there.'

Jeremy James felt something cold and wet slither against his foot, and when he looked down, there was water coming over his toes. Even though he was standing on the right side of the flag, he had a funny feeling that the tide could still catch him, and he took a big step backwards.

'You're scared,' said Timothy, and took a big step forwards. 'I'm on the other side now, but I haven't been caught, have I? Look!' He took another step. And then another. There was a loud squelch every time he lifted his foot out of the sticky mud, but Jeremy James had to admit that Timothy seemed very un-caught at the moment.

'Are you coming?' called Timothy. 'Or are you too scared?'

'I'm not scared!' said Jeremy James.

'Come on then!' said Timothy.

The trouble with grown-ups is that sometimes they're right and sometimes they're wrong, but there's no way of knowing which type of sometimes it is. So did the tide catch people, or didn't it? Well, it hadn't caught Timothy. There he was, jumping around a long way from the red flag, and he actually seemed to be enjoying himself. People don't enjoy themselves when they're being caught by the tide, do they? But if Mummy was right, Timothy might stop enjoying himself.

Jeremy James looked round to see if there was a grown-up he could ask. 'Excuse me,' he would say, 'but is it true that the tide catches people if they go past the red flag?' Then the grown-up would either say yes, and Jeremy James would be the world champion know-all, or no, in which case he could go leaping into the water and Timothy couldn't accuse him of being scared.

But there were no grown-ups to ask. Timothy and Jeremy James were completely alone by the red flags.

'You're scared!' shouted Timothy.

Jeremy James frowned. This was a real problem. If you're scared, how do you appear unscared without doing the thing you're scared of? Jeremy James thought hard and then harder. And suddenly his frown cleared, his head rose, and his heart lightened.

'I've just got to go and see about something!' he shouted, and before Timothy could shout back, Jeremy James was racing away from the sea and towards Mummy and Daddy. After all, no one can be accused of being scared when they've got to see about something. Seeing about something is much more important than jumping around in the sea. And there was no way Timothy could know that the something Jeremy James was seeing about was nothing.

Daddy had just taken off his vest, shoes and socks when Jeremy James finished breaking the world record for that particular stretch of beach.

'Hullo, Jeremy James,' said Daddy. 'I was just coming to get you. You've saved me the trouble.'

'Oooh, is it teatime?' asked Jeremy James.

'All he ever thinks about is his stomach,' said Mummy.

'No I don't,' said Jeremy James, 'I think about chocolate and ice creams and strawberries...'

'Actually,' said Daddy, 'I was coming to bring you away from those red flags. Didn't Mummy tell you it was dangerous to play round there?'

'Yes,' said Jeremy James, 'but I didn't go past them. Timothy did, but I didn't.'

'Was that Timothy from next door?' asked Daddy.

'Yes,' said Jeremy James. 'Worse luck!'

'Where is he now, then?' asked Daddy.

'He's still out there,' said Jeremy James. 'I told him he'd get caught by the tide, but he didn't believe me.'

'He's in the sea?' said Daddy. 'Are you sure?'

'Yes,' said Jeremy James.

'Come on,' said Daddy. 'You'd better show me where he is.'

Jeremy James started to run down the beach with Daddy, pointing to the flag where Timothy had gone into the water, and then Daddy rushed away from him as if he'd been fired from a rocket. Jeremy James had never seen Daddy move at such speed. If Daddy had been chased by a bull, he couldn't have run any faster than he was running now. Jeremy James's world record for that particular stretch of beach was totally shattered as Daddy hurtled past the red flag and into the water. Jeremy James watched him splashing and squelching, and the water was up to his ankles, his shins, his knees ... and still Daddy went on. And then Jeremy James saw and heard what Daddy was splashing towards. Standing in the sea, with water right up to his chest, was Timothy, and he was shouting and crying at the same time.

'Hold on!' called Daddy. 'I'm coming!'

'Help, blubber, blubber, help!' came

the sound of Timothy's voice.

Daddy caught hold of him, swept him
up in his arms, and carried him back out

of the sea. Timothy was twitching like a fish, and his mouth was a bit like a fish's too, opening and shutting and turned right down at both corners.

As Daddy walked back up the beach with Timothy in his arms, and with Jeremy James at his side, Mrs Smyth-Fortescue came running to meet them.

'What happened?' she cried.

'He's all right, Mrs Smyth-Fortescue,' said Daddy, 'he had a bit of a scare, that's all. You're all right now, aren't you, Timothy?'

But Timothy was still too busy shivering and crying to be able to say whether he was all right or not. He clung to Daddy like a limpet to a rock, and Daddy offered to carry him back to the hotel, which Mrs Smyth-Fortescue said was not far away.

'You ought to know,' said Daddy, as the four of them went up the steps and away from the beach, 'that if it hadn't been for Jeremy James, your son might not have lived to tell the tale.'

'What happened, Jeremy?' asked Mrs Smyth-Fortescue.

'Jeremy *James*,' said Jeremy James.

'Well, I told him not to go past the red flags or the tide would catch him, but he didn't believe me. Because he doesn't know very much, you see. So I went and told Daddy that Timothy was in the water.'

'I don't know how to thank you,' Mrs Smyth-Fortescue said. 'You saved Timothy's life.'

By now they had reached the hotel, which was one of those along the front. Mrs Smyth-Fortescue took a pound coin out of her purse and gave it to Jeremy James.

'Thank you!' said Jeremy James, beginning to enjoy life-saving. 'That's my second treasure in two days!'

'Isn't your husband here, Mrs Smyth-Fortescue?' asked Daddy.

'No, he's away on business,' said Mrs Smyth-Fortescue. 'It's just Timothy and me here at the moment.'

'Well,' said Jeremy James, 'I don't think you should let Timothy play on his own again. I might not always be able to save his life.'

At this moment Mrs Smyth-Fortescue was taking Timothy out of Daddy's arms. Timothy raised his tear-lined face and poked his tongue out at Jeremy James. Jeremy James poked out his own tongue and waved the pound coin in the air.

Mrs Smyth-Fortescue thanked Daddy and Jeremy James again, then went into the hotel, carrying Timothy up against her shoulder.

'What was the name of that hotel?' Jeremy James asked Daddy as they walked back to the beach.

'Ocean View,' said Daddy. 'Why?'

'I thought so,' said Jeremy James. 'He wasn't even staying at the Grandmother Polly Ann.'

CHAPTER TEN

MONKEYS AND LIONS

It was the last day of the holiday. Jeremy James looked sadly out of the car window at the sea, the trampolines and the merry-go-round. He could see the donkeys trudging along the beach, led by the young man in the straw hat, and he wondered if Speedy was walking or standing still today. The sun was shining, the sand was golden, the sky was blue, and it was a perfect day not to end a holiday.

'Can't we leave tomorrow instead?' asked Jeremy James.

'Daddy has to work,' said Mummy.

'Who invented work?' asked Jeremy James.

'Nobody invented it,' said Mummy. 'It's just there and has to be done.'

'Well, I wish someone would invent an unwork,' said Jeremy James, 'so that we could stay on holiday.'

But nobody invented an unwork in

110

time to keep Jeremy James at Warkin-on-Sea, and away they went in the direction of what was to be the final treat of the holiday. They were heading for a safari park. Mummy explained to Jeremy James that this was something like a zoo, but instead of people wandering around looking at the animals, the animals wandered around looking at the people. There would be elephants and lions and tigers, and the people sat in their cars while the animals walked free.

The safari park sounded exciting, and when eventually the car drew up at the ticket office, even the twins were happily cooing away like two pigeons on an elephant's back.

The ticket man looked through the window. 'You're not going to feed them to the lions, are you?' he said to Jeremy James.

'Oh no,' said Jeremy James, 'you're not allowed to feed animals in the zoo.'

When the car drove off again, Jeremy James watched out eagerly for lions amid the trees and bushes. But all he saw was a few cows in a field.

'They're not lions!' he said. 'They're cows!'

'Did you know,' said Daddy, 'that cows eat lions?'

'They don't!' said Jeremy James. 'Do they?'

'Yes, they do,' said Daddy. 'Dandelions.'

'Don't tease,' said Mummy. 'We haven't got to the lion reserve yet. Oh look!'

Through the windscreen Jeremy James saw a leopard skin on stilts. It was only when the stilts began to stalk slowly away that Jeremy James realized it was a giraffe. Then he noticed more giraffes, and some zebras too, grazing at the side of the road. One of them actually walked out in front of the car, and Daddy stopped.

'Always stop at a zebra crossing,' he murmured, and Mummy laughed.

When they had seen enough of the giraffes and zebras, they drove on to the next enclosure, where there were rhinos and elephants. Elephants were Jeremy James's favourite animals, but these elephants proved to be rather boring.

They did nothing but snuffle up bundles of hay, and the rhinos were no better, because they just munched away at the grass. And so when it became clear that they were not going to push over a tree or charge at each other or sit on a car and do a Number Two, Jeremy James asked Daddy to move to the next field.

'Monkeys!' said Mummy, with a tone of delight.

'Monkeys!' said Jeremy James, with a tone of disgust.

Mummy and Daddy loved monkeys and thought they were very clever, but Jeremy James thought they were just boring. They couldn't do anything that he couldn't do twice as well, and besides they always had nasty sore-looking bottoms. It was bad enough that they were boring, but it was even worse if you had to look at their sore red bottoms.

'Just look at that!' said Daddy.

As there was nothing else to do, Jeremy James followed Daddy's outstretched arm, looked, and looked again. There were about a dozen monkeys climbing all over a red car. In the red car was a little boy who was laughing, a Mummy who was looking frightened, and a Daddy who was looking furious. The Daddy was hooting, and banging on his windscreen, and trying hard to drive on, though he had to keep stopping because of the monkeys on the bonnet. The monkeys were not just climbing over the car, they were actually pulling bits off it. Jeremy James watched with fascination as one monkey got hold of a strip of silvery metal along the side of the car, and pulled it right away. Another was sitting on the wing tugging the car aerial, and others were playing with the bumpers and wing mirrors.

'Lucky people,' thought Jeremy

James.

'Poor people,' said Mummy. 'We ought to try and help them.'

Daddy drew up alongside the other car, and shouted through the closed window: 'We'll get help!'

The Daddy in the other car waved and said 'Thank you!'

Then before the monkeys could even think of jumping on Daddy's car, he had driven away again like a lunatic on the motorway.

'Oh, can't we stay?' said Jeremy James, with a tone of disappointment.

'I thought you didn't like monkeys,' said Mummy.

'I like *those* monkeys,' said Jeremy James. 'I've never seen monkeys eating cars before!'

But grown-ups are never interested in interesting things, and so even the car-eating monkeys had to be left behind as quickly as possible. In fact, Daddy only slowed down when he caught sight of a black-and-white striped land-rover ('Are they pretending to be zebras, Daddy?') which he hooted at until it came driving across. Then both vehicles stopped. Daddy told the driver about the car-eating monkeys, and the zebra-striped land-rover headed back to the monkey field.

Jeremy James watched it go, and when he next looked to the front, they were passing through some heavy iron gates, which the attendant closed as soon as they were clear.

'Lion country,' murmured Daddy. 'This should be interesting.'

And interesting it was, though not quite in the way Daddy meant. The first bit of excitement came when they spotted a whole pride of lions right by the roadside, tearing great chunks of meat to pieces. Daddy stopped the car, and they watched the jaws and the paws and the claws at work, cracking, crunching, scratching and scrunching away. Then it became even more exciting when a huge, shaggy-maned lion came strolling up to the car and looked through the window straight into Jeremy James's eyes.

'Gosh,' said Jeremy James, 'if I opened the window now, I could actually touch him.'

'If you opened the window now,' said Daddy, 'he could actually touch you.'
'Let's move on,' said Mummy. 'I don't

like them so close.'

Jeremy James could hardly believe his ears. Surely not even a grown-up could want to go away when there was a lion just outside the window. He could clearly see the yellowish flecks in its eyes, and the blood and slaver on its jaws. No one could possibly have ever been so close to a lion before. Mummy *couldn't* want to go away.

But Mummy did. 'Go on, John,' she said. 'Start the car.'

It was at this moment that lion country became extra exciting. Daddy did try to start the car. And the car gave a wheezy snort, like a lion with indigestion, and remained where it was. Daddy tried again, and again there was a whirr, cough and splutter, followed by silence. The lion wandered round to Mummy's side of the car and peered in at her and the twins, licking its lips as if about to eat a giant ice cream.

'John!' cried Mummy. 'Get us out of here!'

'I can't,' said Daddy. 'It won't start.'

Some of the other lions began to look with interest at the whirring, coughing, spluttering creature that was sitting right beside them. Two of them got up and wandered across to have a closer look, so that there were now three lions circling Daddy's car.

'Hoot them!' said Mummy. And so Daddy put his hand on the hooter and pressed. The two new lions took no notice at all, but the first lion, who was still gazing hungrily at Mummy and the twins, jumped back and gave an angry roar. Evidently there was nothing in the Lions' Guide to Human Behaviour to indicate the existence of such a strange sound. But although Daddy hooted again, he still wouldn't go away.

'This *is* exciting,' said Jeremy James. 'Do you think we can sleep here, too? With the lions?'

'I'd die of fright,' said Mummy. 'John, what are we going to do?'

At that moment, a car drew up alongside them. It was a red car, and it had a broken aerial and bits of metal sticking out all over. The little boy inside was laughing, and he waved to Jeremy James, who waved back. The Mummy looked worried, and the Daddy was making signals with his arm.

'Are you stuck?' he shouted through the closed window.

'Yes!' Daddy shouted back.

'We'll get help!' shouted the other man.

'Thank you!' shouted Daddy.

The red car drove off, and Mummy gave a sigh of relief.

'Does that mean we shan't be staying?' asked Jeremy James.

'That's right,' said Daddy. 'We're going to be rescued. Save your neighbour from the monkeys, and he'll rescue you from the lions. Old Warkin proverb.'

Sure enough, in just a few minutes' time there were two zebra-striped land-rovers charging to the rescue. One of them chased away the lions, while the driver from the second attached a rope to Daddy's car and then towed it out of the lion enclosure, and into a big yard where there were several cars and some more land-rovers.

'Thank heaven that's over!' said Mummy.

Jeremy James shook his head. 'I don't

think I'll ever understand grown-ups!' he
said out loud.

'And I shall never understand lion-
tamers!' said Mummy.

'And I shall never understand motor
cars!' said Daddy.

Daddy and Jeremy James got out of
the car, and while Daddy watched a man
fiddling with the engine, Jeremy James
watched for the lion he hoped would
come roaring into the yard. But the only
roar was that of the engine, and the
fiddling man straightened up and told
Daddy: 'She'll be all right now, sir. Just
the old worple worples got a bit over-
heated.'

Once again the family settled down in

the car, and once again Jeremy James gazed sadly out of the window as they left the car-eating monkeys and the man-eating lions further and further behind. Then suddenly they were back on the motorway, amid the same old lunatics and middle-lane-huggers they had raced on the way to Warkin. Jeremy James sank back in his seat and closed his eyes. The next thing he knew was that Mummy was bending over him, shaking him gently and saying: 'We're home, Jeremy James. We're home.' And when he looked out of the window, there it was—their very own house, just the same as when they'd left it such a long time ago. Jeremy James scrambled out of his seat, jumped out of the car, and rushed to the front door where he waited impatiently for Daddy to come and turn the key.

As he entered the hall, Jeremy James felt almost as if the house put its arms out to greet him.

'I'll bet the house was lonely without us,' he said.

Then he ran upstairs to look at his room, and everything there was warm and welcoming. Even his favourite teddy bear was lying in bed quietly waiting for him. The pictures on the walls were still the same, and the cupboard and chair were the same, too. They were like old friends, and Jeremy James knew they were as pleased to see him as he was to see them.

'Well, Jeremy James,' said Mummy, when they were all sitting round the table eating their supper. 'Did you enjoy your holiday?'

'Yes, thank you,' said Jeremy James. 'But it *is* nice to be home again.'

'Wouldn't you prefer to live at Mrs Gullick's?' asked Mummy.

'No, thank you,' said Jeremy James.

'Or Warkin Castle, or the totty-botty hotel?' asked Daddy. 'Or the safari park?'

'No,' said Jeremy James. 'I liked Mrs Gullick's, and the hotel. And I liked the safari park. I liked the safari park a lot. I think all those places are very nice. But I think home is really the nicest place of all.'